PUFFIN BOOKS

Milly of the Rovers

Harriet Castor grew up in Warwickshire, where she went to a full-time dancing school. She has been writing stories for as long as she can remember, and wrote her first Puffin book, *Fat Puss and Friends*, at the age of twelve. After graduating from Cambridge University with a degree in History, she lived in Prague for a while, teaching English and getting lost on trams. Returning to Britain, she spent the next few years as an editor in children's publishing, but now writes full time. She lives in Oxfordshire with a rather nice person called John and one very rascally kitten.

Some other books by Harriet Castor

FAT PUSS AND FRIENDS
FAT PUSS ON WHEELS
FAT PUSS AND SLIMPUP

HARRIET CASTOR
Milly of the Rovers

352254

Illustrated by Christyan Fox

PUFFIN BOOKS

PUFFIN BOOKS

Published by the Penguin Group
Penguin Books Ltd, 27 Wrights Lane, London W8 5TZ, England
Penguin Putnam Inc., 375 Hudson Street, New York, New York 10014, USA
Penguin Books Australia Ltd, Ringwood, Victoria, Australia
Penguin Books Canada Ltd, 10 Alcorn Avenue, Toronto, Ontario, Canada M4V 3B2
Penguin Books (NZ) Ltd, 182–190 Wairau Road, Auckland 10, New Zealand

Penguin Books Ltd, Registered Offices: Harmondsworth, Middlesex, England

First published by Viking 1996
Published in Puffin Books 1998
3 5 7 9 10 8 6 4 2

Filmset in 14/22 Palatino

Made and printed in England by Clays Ltd, St Ives plc

British Library Cataloguing in Publication Data
A CIP catalogue record for this book is available from the British Library

ISBN 0–140–37839–1

*For the old Regent's Park mid-week mixed team –
and for J. B., the best footballer I know*

Contents

1. Sal's Salon

SWOOOOSH!

The ball whizzed through the air and landed at Milly's feet. YEARRGGH! went the crowd, thumping the air in approval.

"And Milly Hawkins is on the ball, Jeff. She's making a run for it down the left wing."

"Just look at her go, Dave! The best striker in the world today – what a pleasure to watch!"

"Yes, Jeff, and what a run this is! A dummy, a swerve, and the Brazilian defence is all over the place."

"They won't be happy with this one, Dave. The goalkeeper's off his line . . . but Hawkins has bamboozled him and –"

"GOAL!!!!!!"

"In-cred-ible!"

All around the stadium, thousands of voices started chanting:

"MIL-LY! MIL-LY! MIL-LY!"

"Milly! *Milly!*"

A familiar voice broke into Milly's dream.

"What are you doing to Mrs Fotherington-Smythe's hair?"

"Oops."

Milly's mother snatched away the comb and hairdryer. She looked very cross.

"Honestly, my girl, you'll never make a good hairdresser if you can't concentrate. Fetch the broom and sweep up the clippings."

"Sorry, Mum."

It was a Friday after school and Milly was helping out at her mother's salon.

She was supposed to be learning how to be a hairdresser, but all Milly really wanted to do was play football.

"Stupid game," her mother always said when Milly told her. "It's a waste of time."

The shop was called Sal's Salon. This wasn't after Milly's mother – her name was Jennifer. Milly didn't know who 'Sal' was.

Sal's Salon had pink peeling wallpaper and big pink chairs that you could pump up and down with a foot pedal. It was quite fun. But it wasn't a patch on a game of –

"Broom!" said Milly's mother.

"Right-ho," said Milly, and went to get it.

She tried very hard to concentrate on

what she was doing.

She even tried listening in to Mrs Fotherington-Smythe's conversation –

". . . new Council Leader, Dr Pinch . . . blah, blah, blah . . . she's a real new broom, Horace says . . . blah, blah, blah . . . has a bee in her bonnet . . ."

– but it was so boring.

". . . about making this town a success . . . going to shut down any hospitals, shops or schools that aren't glamorous enough, she says . . . You'd better watch out yourself, Jennifer – she'll be checking up on Sal's Salon, too."

Milly's mum laughed nervously. But Milly didn't notice. In her head, she was already back at Wembley.

2. Milly's Left Foot

What Milly's mother didn't realize was
that although Milly looked like an
ordinary girl – she wasn't one.

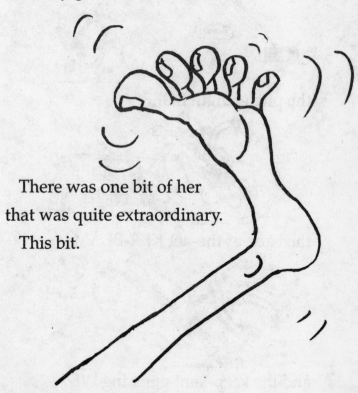

There was one bit of her
that was quite extraordinary.
This bit.

Milly's left foot was amazing. It was the best footballing foot in the whole of Grimethorpe Combined School, capable of things other feet could only dream of.

Things like

the pitch-length BOFF

the back-of-the-net KER-BLAM

and the keep-'em'-guessing WIZ-

FIDDLE.

Sadly, Milly's right foot wasn't so good. In fact, when it came to kicking a ball, Milly's right foot was the wrong foot. It was about as useful as a piece of fudge.

This wouldn't have been a problem, except that Milly couldn't tell left from right. There she'd be, in the middle of a match, on-line for scoring the best goal of the season – she'd take a swing . . .

. . . and the ball would dribble off in completely the wrong direction.

"Bother!"

It was very frustrating.

But Milly was going to be a footballing legend, of that she was absolutely certain.

And one day, somehow, she and her school team, Grimethorpe Rovers, were going to be heroes. That would stop her mum calling football a waste of time!

There was just one problem. Grimethorpe Rovers never won anything.

They were quite possibly the worst football team in history, and they were the laughing stock of Grimethorpe Combined School.

Even Milly had to admit that the line-up wasn't promising:

There were the triplets, Shaz, Kaz and Maz. They always insisted on running everywhere together. Which wouldn't have been a problem, except that they always ran AWAY from the ball.

People ...... can't tell ...... us apart...

There was Duncan
from Class 2, who was
brilliant at dribbling
. . . just not the sort you
do with your feet.

There was Polly, who couldn't see
where the other players were, let alone
the ball . . .

and Alan, the
goalie, who was
keen – but on
gymnastics,
not football.

Then there was
Colin, who was
allergic to everything,

Trevor, who could
trip himself up without
help from anyone else,

..oops!

BOING!

Cress, who was very
talented with
chewing-gum – but
not with a football,

and Nigel, who always fell asleep at
matches – even when he was on the ball.

Last but not least, there was the captain:
Milly herself. Just last Saturday she'd
been racing towards goal at a million
miles an hour . . .

She'd got past
one tackle,

two tackles,

three tackles,

and when the coast was clear, and she'd
sorted out (for once) which foot was
which –

POW! – she'd slammed the ball into the
back of the net.

It was only when she'd been halfway
through her Darren Dangerfoot victory

knee-slide that she'd realized it was actually the wrong net . . . and it was her own team who'd been trying to stop her.

"Milly!"

"Sorry."

No – if Milly's mum, and the rest of the world, were ever going to take Grimethorpe Rovers seriously, they were going to have to shape up.

But how?

3. A Problem for Mr Bute

Hello..? Bute here...

HEADMASTER

Brrriiinnnggg!

That same Friday night, the phone rang in the office of Mr Bute, the headmaster of Grimethorpe Combined.

"Hello?" he said, picking up the receiver.

"Bute?" snapped a voice. "It's Pinch here. Dr Pinch – the new Council Leader."

"Oh, how nice -" began Mr Bute.

"I've just got one thing to say to you, Bute," Dr Pinch interrupted. "And that's: SUCCESS."

"S-success?" stammered Mr Bute, feeling rather flustered.

"That's what I said," replied Dr Pinch. "There's no room for failures in this town. It's new Council policy. If anything's a failure, we'll get rid of it. And of all the failures I can see around here –" (she frowned at her secretary, who went scurrying out of the room) "– of all the failures I can see around here, Bute, Grimethorpe Combined is the biggest."

Dr Pinch swung her chair round to face the massive wall-map pinned up behind her, and jabbed at it with her pointer as she talked.

"There are two schools in this town," she explained, as though Mr Bute didn't know already. "Grimethorpe and Redlands. This town isn't big enough for two schools. It doesn't need two schools. It's wasteful. It's greedy. It's lax and lardy. It's uneconomical. One of them must go. And it's my job to decide which one."

Mr Bute gulped. If it was Grimethorpe versus Redlands, Grimethorpe wouldn't stand a chance.

"Streamlined. Sleek. Smart. These are words we like, Bute. But these are not words we can use to describe Grimethorpe Combined, now, can we?"

Mr Bute, slumped in his chair, surveyed his office miserably. No – the sagging beanbags, the scatter-cushions, the pictures of Mrs Bute and little Ruby – none of them were what you might call streamlined. Or smart.

Dr Pinch was still talking. "A fortnight, Bute. That's what you have. Two weeks. Fourteen days. Three hundred and thirty-six hours. And then there will be a meeting of the Council's new 'One School' committee, which I've just set up –" (actually she'd only just thought of it) "– and we will be deciding which school stays open and which school shuts down. In the meantime, my inspectors will be coming round to investigate."

Mr Bute heard her ring off. He stared into space for several seconds, listening to the dialling tone. Then he slowly replaced the receiver.

Just five minutes ago, he'd been a happy man. He'd been about to go home to a lovely comfy evening with his family, looking forward to the next week at his comfy, happy school. And now . . . now he felt like one of his beanbags. He had lost his stuffing.

He got out of his chair and reached for his coat. He'd have to find another job. He couldn't work for that awful headmaster, Mr Slimjim, at Redlands – it didn't bear thinking about. No, he'd have to give up teaching altogether.

And Mr Bute, who never usually felt the cold, pulled his overcoat tightly around him, and shivered as he made his way out into the night.

4. Just Another Match

The next day, Grimethorpe Rovers had their last but one match of the season. It was against Ruffemup United, a team in the next town.

As usual, the Rovers went there in the team bus, a rusty old contraption held together by three bootlaces and a skipping-rope. It had red plastic seats that stuck to your legs on hot days, and it smelt unmistakably of DOG.

The dog in question was called Punter.
He belonged to Mr Beagley, the school
caretaker and bus driver. Punter looked
something like a cross between an old
bathmat and a dish mop, and he smelt
like he'd been rolling in oily puddles for
several days. Which he probably had.

But, despite being the smelliest, hairiest

35

dog in the world, Punter was also the Rovers' best, most loyal and ONLY supporter.

You could spot him on the touchline at every single Grimethorpe match and you could spot his hairs at every match all over the Grimethorpe kit.

Today was no different. In fact it was, altogether, quite a usual sort of Saturday.

Alan the goalie spent his time practising handstands against the cross-bar.

Colin went for a header and found he was allergic to the ball. And Milly forgot to change direction after half-time and scored another own-goal.

Ruffemup United were all little squits, but they were as hard as nails and liked proving it.

They got fifteen goals.

Grimethorpe Rovers got none. But they did get

three grazed knees

five bruised ankles

one black eye

and a new-look strip.

Yep, thought Milly as the bus spluttered
homewards. Just a usual sort of Saturday.

5. SUCCESS

On Monday morning, Mr Bute went to assembly with a heavy heart. As soon as the Grimethorpe pupils saw him, they knew that something was wrong. Usually he sat on the edge of the stage, swinging his legs and cracking jokes. But this morning he stood up, ramrod straight, and tried very hard to look stern. He gave a long talk about doing your best, and polishing your shoes and being streamlined (whatever that meant), and

he held up a big notice with SUCCESS written on it. But you could tell his heart wasn't in it; he'd spelt it wrong.

"It's no use," he said at last. "We're done for."

"What do you mean, Mr B?" piped up Shona McVale, who was in Milly's class. Shona was going to be a reporter – the sort who interviews the big stars. For now, though, Shona was making do with running the school magazine, the *Grimethorpe Times*.

"Well, Shona, it's like this –" began Mr Bute. And he told her all about Dr Pinch's plans to shut down one of the town's schools.

And about how the inspectors were going to come round to measure which school was the most successful.

And about how, if Grimethorpe was

shut down, all the Grimethorpe pupils
would have to go to Redlands instead.

And, at this, some of the infants turned
pale and started crying, and the juniors
reached for their catapults and their
super-ballistic homemade pea–shooters.

To have to go to Redlands – it was a fate

worse than . . . well, than compulsory
Cheese Pie for school dinner every day
for a whole year.

Why was it so bad? You just had to take
a look at the Redlanders to see why.

They had a sharp, cut-and-thrust look in
their eyes, and a proud tilt to their noses.
Their shoelaces were ironed, their hair
was polished, and
they could recite
the thirteen times
table backwards
at the drop of a
hat.

They were also
the meanest,
cheatingest,
break-every-rule
skunks in the
world. But just
because they

always looked squeaky clean and lickety-
split tidy, the people in Milly's town
always said:

While, even though Grimethorpers
were the bravest, most fearless, against-
all-the-odds good guys 'n' gals in the
world, the townsfolk said:

Everything bad that Redlanders did, Grimethorpers got blamed for it. No wonder they hated each other.

"There's nothing else for it," said Mr Bute, looking round the hall. "We'll just have to try our best to be the most successful school."

And try their best they certainly did.

All that day, Grimethorpe pupils were busy polishing, cleaning and sprucing. Cushions were plumped, sofas were swept, and cracks were hidden behind brand new posters. Even Punter was given a bath – though he went straight back to his favourite oily puddle afterwards.

By the time Dr Pinch's inspectors – Inspector Slicer, Inspector Nettle and Inspector Trim – turned up the next morning, Grimethorpe Combined School had taken on a new lease of life.

And that included the pupils, too. They'd polished their satchels and pulled up their socks, and whenever an inspector was nearby, they made sure they talked loudly about very complicated long division sums.

Even Mr Bute made a special effort to wear shirts and ties that didn't clash. He found it rather tricky.

6. Dr Pinch has a Plan

All week, the inspectors at Grimethorpe and the inspectors at Redlands ticked and crossed, and measured and weighed, and sniffed the air for the scent of success.

By Friday, Dr Pinch was not pleased. Worse than that – Dr Pinch was furious. Because somehow – and how she didn't quite know – Grimethorpe and Redlands had got equal points. They were neck and neck.

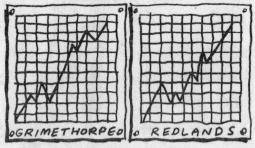

Now, despite what she'd said to Mr Bute, Dr Pinch wasn't truly interested in finding out which school she should close – she'd already decided. Whatever the inspectors' reports said, Dr Pinch wanted to shut down Grimethorpe Combined.

She didn't like Grimethorpe. It was a comfy, happy place, and comfiness and happiness were two of the things that Dr Pinch hated most of all.

But there was another reason, too – one that no one else knew about. It was a secret locked away in Dr Pinch's rather cold, hard heart. And the secret was that she had fallen in love with Mr Slimjim, the Redlands headmaster.

So if – she shuddered to think of it – if Grimethorpe actually won the contest and she had to shut down Redlands, it would be a disaster! Her Slimjim – in disgrace!

No – Redlands had to win. And Dr
Pinch had to find some way to make sure
that they did.

So she came up with a plan.

Dr Pinch's plan came to her late that
night when she was lying in the bath, and
she thought it was a particularly brilliant

one. It was this: since the scores were level, there would have to be a tie-break. And, to make completely sure that Redlands would win it, she had decided that the tie-break should be a football match. Or, more precisely, should be the Grudge Cup match that was due to be played the next Saturday.

The Grudge Cup was a once-a-year football match between Grimethorpe Rovers and Dynamo Redlands. It was the last match of the season and, for the Rovers, it was the worst.

In all the fifty-three years since the Grudge Cup had been invented, Grimethorpe had won it just once. That was the year there was a freak storm at half-time and all the Redlands players were struck by lightning.

Every other year, the Rovers hadn't stood a chance.

"Excellent!" thought Dr Pinch to herself. "My darling Slimjim's school will have no problem beating that bunch of losers."

7. The Challenge

The next day, Mr Bute had another phone call from Dr Pinch, telling him about the tie-break. As soon as he had put the phone down, he pressed the button on his intercom.

"Miss Marchmount?" he said into the speaker. "Miss Marchmount – please bring me Milly Hawkins from Class 3. I need to speak to her urgently."

A second later Miss Marchmount, carried at lightning speed by her new SpringStep training shoes, had reached Class 3 – just at the moment when Milly had mixed up the test tube in her right hand with the test tube in her left hand, and had managed to make the world's first double choc-chip stink bomb

explode. It was lucky that none of the
inspectors were observing Class 3's
science lesson that morning.

"Milly," said Miss Marchmount, wiping burnt hundreds and thousands off her glasses, "Mr Bute needs to see you straightaway."

"Right-ho," said Milly.

Mr Bute decided not to ask why Milly looked like a large hot fudge sundae. He got on with what he had to say.

He explained about the tie-break. And how the Rovers were going to have to win the Grudge Cup.

"Win?" said Milly. "*Win?* You mean actually get more goals than Dynamo Redlands?"

"I'm afraid so," said Mr Bute.

"But . . . but . . ." Milly spluttered. The Dynamo Redlands players were the biggest, meanest bruisers in the footballing universe. Playing against them was like getting run over by a steamroller. And what's more, though their playing was dirty, just because their kit was clean the ref never seemed to notice.

Now, if Mr Bute had asked Grimethorpe Rovers to beat Brazil, or AC Milan, it mightn't have been so bad . . . but Dynamo Redlands? It was impossible.

"Have we got time to buy in players from anywhere else?" asked Milly, thinking of those big transfer deals she was always hearing about on the telly. "Like Manchester United, or Arsenal, or – or Liverpool?"

Mr Bute smiled sadly. "I don't think so," he said. "We'll just have to make do with what we've got."

Milly swallowed. Mr Bute was looking at her earnestly. Footballing legends, Milly reminded herself, don't bottle out.

"We'll give it a go, Mr Bute," she said firmly. Then she fainted.

8. Inspiration

At break, Milly went to talk to Punter. She
found him round the back of Mr
Beagley's office (which was actually a
shed), playing dead lions.

"What am I going to do, Punter?" she asked him, staring deep into the fluff and wondering where his eyes were.

Punter slurped her on the nose. It wasn't much help.

The fact was, Milly had already tried everything she could think of to make Grimethorpe Rovers into a lean, mean fighting machine.

She'd tried training sessions.

There'd been the early morning runs that only she and Punter had turned up to.

Then there'd been the early morning runs that even Punter hadn't turned up to.

Then there'd been that exercise session. At the next match, everyone had been so stiff they'd hardly been able to move at all.

She'd tried tactics, too. She'd come up with all sorts of clever plans, and drawn them out in complicated diagrams. But at the team talk before the next match she'd ended up, as usual, having to explain the rules of the game to some of the players who'd forgotten since last week.

And the one time they'd tried out different formations on the pitch it'd looked more like *Come Dancing* than *Match of the Day*.

It was no use. Milly had run out of ideas. Just when the Rovers – and Grimethorpe – needed her most.

She ruffled Punter's fluff and went sadly back into school. Her mother was right – perhaps she'd have to be a hairdresser after all.

But then that night, Milly had a strange dream.

She was back in Mr Bute's office. But instead of Mr Bute sitting behind the desk, there was Milly's footballing hero, Darren Dangerfoot. And he was saying one thing to her, over and over again.

"We'll have to make do with what we've got. We'll have to . . ."

Milly woke up with a start. "A-ha!" she said out loud.

She had just had the most wonderful idea.

9. Secret Weapons

The next day, strange things started happening at Grimethorpe Combined School. Odd noises were heard coming from behind Mr Beagley's shed.

Milly was seen running around with a very large roll of sticky-tape.

And Nigel was several times spotted almost awake, even in lessons.

It was all very mysterious. The Rovers were in training, but this wasn't the sort of training anyone had ever seen before.

And quite what it had to do with a
game of football, nobody was sure.

"It's no use hoping we'll all turn into
Darren Dangerfoot," said Milly when
Shona asked her for a pre-match
interview. "But we've each got talents –

and we're going to use them. No further comment."

Even Shona was confused.

"Talents?"

The day before the big match, Milly ran straight home from school to practise in the back yard.

She'd perfected the new Hawkins Hustle, and her beat-the-best-goalie-in-the-world banana shot wasn't bad either.

Milly had just hit the ball perfectly for the three hundred and ninety-eighth time, when her mother called her in.

Milly! Come here a minute!

Milly's mum was sitting at the kitchen table. She had a letter in one hand, and her piggy bank in the other. She was looking very worried.

"Milly," she said, "I need you to work in the salon tomorrow."

Milly felt her smile crumble. "But Mum!" she cried. "Tomorrow's Saturday!"

"Exactly," said her mother. "So you won't have to miss school."

"No, no – I mean, tomorrow's the Grudge Cup," said Milly frantically.

"I can't miss it. The Rovers have got to win or they'll shut down Grimethorpe. Dr Pinch says so."

Milly's mother sighed. "Well, Dr Pinch has some other things to say as well," she said. And she handed Milly the letter.

"Dear Mrs Hawkins . . ." Dr Pinch had written. "Sal's Salon is a disgrace to the town. It looks a mess. It ought to be shut down. I'll give you until Tuesday to spruce it up – or else you can shut it up. No buts. My word is final. Yours, Dr Prudence Pinch, Council Leader."

"What will you do?" asked Milly.

Her mother shook her head in despair. "I just haven't got enough money to do up the salon – and I can't see how I can get it before Tuesday. Unless – if you work tomorrow, Milly, I can have more customers in, and we might just make enough. It's our only hope."

Milly didn't know what to say.

"If Dr Pinch shuts the salon," her mum went on, "I won't have a job – and I don't know if I'll be able to get another one. At least if Grimethorpe shuts you could go to Redlands."

Milly opened her mouth to say 'Yeuch!', but then she shut it again. She didn't have a choice. She was going to have to miss the match.

10. Grudge Cup Blues

The next morning, Milly was up early, combing and drying, washing and sweeping. But all she could think of was the match.

Nine o'clock – three hours to go before kick-off . . .

two hours to go . . .

one hour . . .

half an hour . . .

It was too much to bear.

Mrs Fotherington-Smythe was in again, and Milly was put in charge of her curlers.

... Horace .. blah, blah, blah... golf club ... blah, blah, blah...

Milly couldn't stand it anymore. She had to do something.

Without stopping to think, she clamped

Mrs Fotherington-Smythe into the big drier, and set it for forty-five minutes each way.

Then she said one last "Yes, Mrs Fotherington-Smythe. How interesting, Mrs Fotherington-Smythe," and slipped out of the back door.

Meanwhile, at the Grimethorpe football pitch, the Dynamo Redlands bus had just glided into view, twinkling in the sunshine. It wasn't much like the Rovers' bus. It had plushy seats and air conditioning, and the name of the local supermarket in glossy letters all down the side. The faces at the window had a cut-and-thrust look in their eyes, and a proud tilt to their noses. Their kit was silky and dog-hair-free.

The bus pulled to a halt, and autograph-hunters crowded round. Out strolled the team, looking relaxed and confident.

Amongst them were . . .

Larry Ginnyka, local hero, and captain of Dynamo Redlands, Mary-Donna, their fiendishly good (and unscrupulous) striker, and Vinny Terribles, the Redlands bully-boy, who specialized in kicking you when the ref wasn't looking.

The Grimethorpe players were already warming up.

But where was Milly? The ref was starting to look edgy.

"We'll have to start without her."

He put the ball on the centre line, tossed a coin to decide who should kick it first and put his whistle in his mouth.

Just then . . .

MILLY!!

Milly had just made it. The ref blew his
whistle, and the match began.

It was tough.

It was muddy.

It was mean.

But by half-time, Dynamo Redlands were worried. This wasn't the Grimethorpe Rovers they knew. If it hadn't been for the tell-tale dog hairs, no one would have recognized Milly and her gang.

The triplets, Shaz, Kaz and Maz, still went everywhere together, but now they had learnt to charge, screaming a blood-curdling war-cry as they went.

Polly was armed with a magnifying glass taped to each lens of her specs giving her SUPER HAWK VISION. The Redlands players didn't know what to do now she wasn't giving them the ball all the time.

In goal, Alan had started putting his best gymnastic skills to good use.

Trevor hadn't stopped tripping over but he HAD learnt to take Vinny Terribles down with him when he fell.

The score so far was 0-0. The Redlands
team were rattled. They were used to
being at least 9-0 up by now. Something
had to be done. The players huddled
close together as they sucked on their
oranges.

Then the whistle blew for the second
half.

It was tougher.

It was muddier.

It was meaner.

But still the Rovers were holding out.

Then Milly noticed Mary-Donna wink
at Vinny, and not in a very nice way.

A few moments later, as soon as the
ref's back was turned, Vinny went for

Trevor, and sent him crashing to the ground.

"That's what you get for messing with me, loser."

"Tripped over his own feet, as usual," said the ref.

Trevor had to be taken off the field.

"We've had it now!" thought Milly. "It's eleven against ten. We've no chance."

No wonder Redlands were suddenly looking happier.

But just then, Milly saw something running on to the pitch. It was Punter!

"A dog as a substitute?" Milly shrugged. "It's got to be better than nothing."

There were only a few minutes of the match to go. The score was still 0-0.

"If we can just hang on a bit longer," thought Milly desperately.

Then, all of a sudden, she spied Punter

with the ball. He was moving faster than she'd ever seen him move in her life.

First he pushed the ball to Duncan's feet . . .

SLOOP!!

. . . then he set off with it along the pitch.

"He won't get far," thought Milly, seeing the Redlands players running up to tackle from all sides. But suddenly they stopped, holding their noses.

Milly gave a yelp of laughter. Beaten by the Punter smell!

79

Punter steadily made his way down the whole field. Milly realized he was heading her way. She got herself into position in front of the goal. Mr Beagley was holding up a sign for her, so she knew it was the right one.

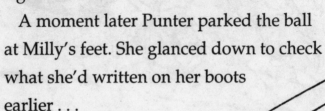

A moment later Punter parked the ball at Milly's feet. She glanced down to check what she'd written on her boots earlier . . .

. . . took a swing, and – POW! – thwacked the ball as hard as she could. It did a perfect banana curve.

The Redlands goalie dived, but, slippery with Duncan's dribble, the ball shot straight through his fingers and landed firmly in the back of the net.

"GOAL!!!!!"

TWANG!

The noise almost drowned out the referee's final whistle.

Milly stood there, her eyes as big as dinner plates and her mouth stretched into the widest grin ever.

1-0! They'd won!

Then suddenly it was mayhem. Grimethorpe pupils were running on to

the pitch, hugging every Rover in sight.
Some even forgot the smell and hugged
Punter. Milly found herself lifted up on to
the players' shoulders and paraded
around like a star.

Grimethorpe was saved! And the
Rovers were footballing heroes – they'd
never be laughed at again!

Meanwhile the Redlanders were
wailing and gnashing their teeth. Now
Redlands would be shut down and they'd
have to go to Grimethorpe. It was a fate
worse than . . . well, worse than
compulsory Cheese Pie for school dinners
for a whole year.

Suddenly, a voice cut through all the
noise.

"Milly Hawkins! Come here at once!
What did you mean by sneaking off like
that? Just look what's happened to Mrs
Fotherington-Smythe's hair!"

It was Milly's mum. And she didn't look pleased.

Milly couldn't help it. She tried very hard not to. But when she opened her mouth to apologize, all that came out was:

"Ha, ha, ha, ha!"

"How can you laugh?" said her mother. "Now we'll have to give Mrs Fotherington-Smythe a refund, and we'll never have enough money by Tuesday. Dr Pinch will shut us down!"

11. Sal's Salon Again

But it didn't come to that. Because the next day, the newspapers reported that straight after the match, Dr Pinch and Mr Slimjim had disappeared together. Someone said they'd run off to get married. But no one found out for certain – because they never came back.

So there was an election for a new Council Leader.

And the winner was Mr Bute.

And Mr Bute declared that he would cancel all Dr Pinch's orders. Everything that she'd been about to shut down, could stay open – and never mind if it didn't look streamlined. Or smart.

Even Redlands should stay open, said Mr Bute. (To be honest, he didn't fancy

having the Redlands pupils in his classes.)
But he appointed a new head for
Redlands, the Reverend Daisychain, who
wasn't like Mr Slimjim at all.

REV. DAISYCHAIN

"This is all thanks to Milly," announced
Mr Bute proudly at assembly the next
week. "And I've been trying to think
what present we could give her as a
reward. Tell me, Milly, what would you
like?"

"Well, there is one thing I can think of,"

said Milly, "but everyone will need to help."

So the next weekend, all the pupils and teachers of Grimethorpe Combined brought ladders and brushes and pots of paint to Sal's Salon. And by Monday morning, it was the shiniest, smartest salon in town.

New customers flocked to see it. Milly's mother had never been so busy.

Soon she had enough money to pay for a proper assistant, called Gerald.

"No, I don't need any help today, Milly," she said each week. "Anyway, haven't you got a football match to go to?"

And, when she had the time, Milly's mum even came to see a few of them.

But, even though Sal's Salon became the most popular place in town, one customer stayed away.

Milly's mother even offered her free haircuts for a year. But it was no use. Mrs Fotherington-Smythe never darkened the door of Sal's Salon again.

"ALL THE WORLD'S A FOOTBALL"

Says Milly Hawkins: Footballing Legend.

A happy Milly Hawkins with the Grudge Cup

Grimethorpe Rovers are justly celebrating a 1-0 victory over Dynamo Redlands. 9 year-old Milly Hawkins, Grimethorpes centre forward said she was "over the moon with the result. In a game of two halves Grimethorpe achieved the right result on the disappeared before the end of the game was said to be as sick as a parrot. Mr. Bute the

Also in Young Puffin

Fat Puss and Friends

Harriet Castor

Fat Puss was fat. He had little thin arms, small flat feet, a very short tail and an amazingly fat tummy.

He can't do all sorts of things that his friends can do, but instead of being miserable he finds some special (and funny) things he *can* do – like making friends with mice!

Also in Young Puffin

FAT PUSS ON WHEELS

Harriet Castor

Fat Puss has fun!

Fat Puss, the roly-poly cat, is up to his old
tricks, and has no end of adventures with
his friends the Mouse family and
Humphrey Beaver. He goes flying, is the
hero of the football match, and roller-skates
into the river!

Join Fat Puss in his funny and
surprising escapades!

Also in Young Puffin

THE *BRAIN-BLASTING ADVENTURES* OF *NORMAN THORMAN*

Lorna Kent

"A terrifying giant tarantula is towering over the shopping centre . . ."

When Norman knocks over his chemistry experiment, little does he know what chaos will follow – his hair begins to sprout and a baby tarantula splashed by the liquid starts to get very large indeed. Can Norman save the day?

Two very entertaining and funny stories about the lovable but accident-prone Norman Thorman, together for the first time in one volume.

The Phantom Knicker Nicker

Jean Ure

**'If someone's nicking Annie's knickers
it's up to us to catch them.'**

The Gang of Four are broke, and setting up
a detective agency seems a great way of
raising extra cash, even if it does mean
guarding old Annie's washing line.

In this funny, entertaining story,
the irrepressible Gang of Four – Priya, Alice,
Vas and Toby – discover that being detectives
is not an easy job!

Also in Young Puffin

GEORGE SPEAKS

Dick King-Smith

Laura's baby brother George was four weeks old when it happened.

George looks like an ordinary baby, with his round red face and squashy nose. But Laura soon discovers that he's absolutely *extraordinary*, and everyone's life is turned upside down from the day George speaks!

Also in Young Puffin

SPORTS DAY
for Charlie
Joy Allen

Sports Day is in two weeks' time

Charlie decides Dad must go on a strict training programme in order to stand any chance of winning the Father's Race. And with Charlie entered for four races, excitement mounts until the big day arrives, and the races are for real.

In the second story, Charlie's class visits a Farm Park. With a football-mad donkey and a pickpocket duck, Charlie finds the trip a brilliant day out.

Together for the first time in one volume, these two stories about Charlie's adventures are fun and easy to read.

Also in Young Puffin

THE REVOLTING BABY

Mary Hooper

Pink from the bath, cross at being parted from Loggy for so long and stuffed into a round puffball of whisper blue, Emily looked revolting.

Katie thinks looking after a baby will be easy. But after Emily has covered herself in sticky golden syrup, newspaper print, scrambled egg, a few leaves and plenty of boot polish, Katie has changed her mind. To complete the picture Emily has become inseparable from her new toy, a very large and dirty log.

Katie is in trouble yet again, in this very funny sequel to *The Revolting Bridesmaid* and *The Revolting Wedding*.

READ MORE IN PUFFIN

For children of all ages, Puffin represents quality and variety – the very best in publishing today around the world.

For complete information about books available from Puffin – and Penguin – and how to order them, contact us at the appropriate address below. Please note that for copyright reasons the selection of books varies from country to country.

On the worldwide web: www.puffin.co.uk

In the United Kingdom: Please write to *Dept. EP, Penguin Books Ltd, Bath Road, Harmondsworth, West Drayton, Middlesex UB7 ODA*

In the United States: Please write to *Consumer Sales, Penguin USA, P.O. Box 999, Dept. 17109, Bergenfield, New Jersey 07621-0120*. VISA and MasterCard holders call 1-800-253-6476 to order Penguin titles

In Canada: Please write to *Penguin Books Canada Ltd, 10 Alcorn Avenue, Suite 300, Toronto, Ontario M4V 3B2*

In Australia: Please write to *Penguin Books Australia Ltd, P.O. Box 257, Ringwood, Victoria 3134*

In New Zealand: Please write to *Penguin Books (NZ) Ltd, Private Bag 102902, North Shore Mail Centre, Auckland 10*

In India: Please write to *Penguin Books India Pvt Ltd, 706 Eros Apartments, 56 Nehru Place, New Delhi 110 019*

In the Netherlands: Please write to *Penguin Books Netherlands bv, Postbus 3507, NL-1001 AH Amsterdam*

In Germany: Please write to *Penguin Books Deutschland GmbH, Metzlerstrasse 26, 60594 Frankfurt am Main*

In Spain: Please write to *Penguin Books S. A., Bravo Murillo 19, 1° B, 28015 Madrid*

In Italy: Please write to *Penguin Italia s.r.l., Via Felice Casati 20, I-20124 Milano.*

In France: Please write to *Penguin France S. A., 17 rue Lejeune, F-31000 Toulouse*

In Japan: Please write to *Penguin Books Japan, Ishikiribashi Building, 2-5-4, Suido, Bunkyo-ku, Tokyo 112*

In South Africa: Please write to *Longman Penguin Southern Africa (Pty) Ltd, Private Bag X08, Bertsham 2013*